CW00863245

THE STORY OF
LITTLE BLACK SAMBO

Pictured By
John R Neill

The Reilly & Lee Co.
Chicago

THE STORY OF
LITTLE BLACK SAMBO

ONCE upon a time there was a little black boy, and his name was Little Black Sambo.

And his Mother was called Black Mumbo.

And his Father was called Black Jumbo.

And Black Mumbo made him a beautiful little Red Coat and a pair of beautiful little Blue Trousers.

Little Black Sambo

And Black Jumbo went to the Bazaar and bought him a beautiful Green Umbrella and a lovely little Pair of Purple Shoes with Crimson Soles and Crimson Linings.

And then wasn't Little Black Sambo grand?

So he put on all his fine clothes and went out for a walk in the Jungle. And by and by he met a Tiger. And the Tiger said to him, "Little Black Sambo, I'm going to eat you up!"

And Little Black Sambo said, "Oh!

Little Black Sambo

Please, Mr. Tiger, don't eat me up, and I'll give you my beautiful little Red Coat." So the Tiger said, "Very well, I won't eat you this time, but you must give me your beautiful little Red Coat." So the Tiger got poor Little Black Sambo's beautiful little Red Coat, and went away saying, "Now I'm the grandest Tiger in the Jungle."

And Little Black Sambo went on, and by and by he met another Tiger, and it said to him, "Little Black Sambo, I'm going to eat you up!" And Little Black

Little Black Sambo

Sambo said, "Oh! Please, Mr. Tiger, don't eat me up, and I'll give you my beautiful little Blue Trousers." So the Tiger said, "Very well, I won't eat you this time, but you must give me your beautiful little Blue Trousers." So the Tiger got poor Little Black Sambo's beautiful little Blue Trousers, and went away saying, "Now I'm the grandest Tiger in the Jungle."

And Little Black Sambo went on, and by and by he met another Tiger, and it said to him, "Little Black Sambo, I'm going to eat you up!" And Little Black Sambo

17

Little Black Sambo

said, "Oh! Please, Mr. Tiger, don't eat me up, and I'll give you my beautiful little Purple Shoes with Crimson Soles and Crimson Linings."

But the Tiger said, "What use would your shoes be to me? I've got four feet, and you've got only two; you haven't got enough shoes for me."

But Little Black Sambo said, "You could wear them on your ears."

"So I could," said the Tiger; "that's a very good idea. Give them to me, and I won't eat you this time."

Little Black Sambo

So the Tiger got poor Little Black Sambo's beautiful little Purple Shoes with Crimson Soles and Crimson Linings, and went away saying, "Now I'm the grandest Tiger in the Jungle."

And by and by Little Black Sambo met another Tiger, and it said to him, "Little Black Sambo, I'm going to eat you up!" And Little Black Sambo said, "Oh, Please, Mr. Tiger, don't eat me up, and I'll give you my beautiful Green Umbrella." But the Tiger said, "How can I carry an umbrella, when I need all my paws for walking with?"

Little Black Sambo

"You could tie a knot in your tail, and carry it that way," said Little Black Sambo. "So I could," said the Tiger. "Give it to me, and I won't eat you this time." So he got poor Little Black Sambo's beautiful Green Umbrella, and went away saying, "Now I'm the grandest Tiger in the Jungle."

And poor Little Black Sambo went away crying, because the cruel Tigers had taken all his fine clothes.

Presently he heard a horrible noise that sounded like "Gr-r-r-r-rrrrrrr," and it got

Little Black Sambo

louder and louder, "Oh, dear!" said Little Black Sambo, "there are all the Tigers coming back to eat me up! What shall I do?" So he ran quickly to a palm-tree and peeped round it to see what the matter was.

And there he saw all the Tigers fighting and disputing which of them was the grandest. And at last they all got so angry that they jumped up and took off all the fine clothes and began to tear each other with their claws, and bite each other with their great big white teeth.

24

Little Black Sambo

And they came, rolling and tumbling right to the foot of the very tree where Little Black Sambo was hiding, but he jumped quickly in behind the umbrella. And the Tigers all caught hold of each others tails as they wrangled and scrambled, and so they found themselves in a ring around the tree.

Then, when he was quite a little distance away from the Tigers, Little Black Sambo jumped up and called out, "Oh! Tigers, why have you taken off all your nice clothes?" Don't you want them any

more?" But the Tigers only answered, "Gr-r-rrrrrr!"

Then Little Black Sambo said, "If you want them, say so, or I'll take them away." But the Tigers would not let go of each others' tails, and so they could only say "Gr-r-r-rrrrrrrr!"

So Little Black Sambo put on all his fine clothes again and walked off.

And the Tigers were very, very angry, but still they would not let go of each others' tails. And they were so angry that they ran round the tree, trying to eat each other up, and they ran faster and faster, till they were whirling round so fast that you couldn't see their legs at all.

And still they ran faster and faster and faster, till they all just melted away, and there was nothing left but a great big pool of melted butter (or "ghi," as it is called in India) round the foot of the tree.

Now Black Jumbo was just coming home from his work, with a great big brass pot in his arms, and when he saw what was left of all the Tigers he said, "Oh! what lovely melted butter!   I'll take that home to Black Mumbo for her to cook with."

So he put it all into the great big brass pot and took it home to Black Mumbo to cook with.

When Black Mumbo saw the melted butter, wasn't she pleased! "Now," said she, "we'll all have pancakes for supper!"

So she got flour and eggs and milk and sugar and butter, and she made a huge big plate of most lovely pancakes. And she fried them in the melted butter which the Tigers had made, and they were just as yellow and brown as little Tigers.

Little Black Sambo

And then they all sat down to supper. And Black Mumbo ate Twenty-seven pancakes, and Black Jumbo ate Fifty-five, but Little Black Sambo ate a Hundred and Sixty nine, because he was so hungry.

THE STORY OF TOPSY
from UNCLE TOM'S CABIN

TOPSY

MANY years ago, when negroes were slaves and were bought and sold the same as horses, cows, chickens or ducks, Mr. Augustine St. Clare, while sauntering about the market place, came upon the blackest little pickaninny girl he had ever seen. She was eight or nine years old, and, besides being very black, had round shining eyes, glittering as glass beads, and

T o p s y

woolly hair braided into little tails, which stuck out in every direction. She was dressed in a filthy, ragged garment and was quite the most woebegone little darkey ever seen by Mr. St. Clare. Perhaps in a spirit of compassion and partly as a joke he bought her and took her home. Her name was Topsy, and when children are old enough they may read all about her in "Uncle Tom's Cabin," a book that had much to do with freeing the slaves; a sad, sad story, indeed; as sad as Topsy, ignorant and care-free, was joyful and mischievous.

The very sight of the scrawny black girl caused Miss Ophelia, Mr. St. Clare's cousin, to throw up her hands in amazement.

"What is it!" she exclaimed.

"I've made a purchase for you," said he, with a grin, looking first at Topsy, whose eyes were bulging wide open at the sight of the fine furniture, and then at his cousin, who had folded her hands in despair.

"Augustine, what in the world did you bring her here for?" protested Miss Ophelia.

"For you to educate, to be sure," he replied, laughingly.

"I thought her a funny little Jim Crow and I bought her. Here, Topsy," he added, whistling as one would call the attention of a puppy dog, "give us a song and show Miss Ophelia how well you can dance."

Topsy's eyes glittered with a kind of wicked drollery, and then, in a clear, shrill voice, she struck up an old negro melody, to which she kept time with her hands and feet, spinning round, clapping her hands, knocking her knees together and shuffling her feet. Finally, she turned two somersaults in front of Miss Ophelia so close

that she almost took the good lady's breath away with amazement.

"Topsy, this is your new mistress," said Mr. St. Clare, solemnly.

"O yes, mas'r," replied Topsy, with another twinkle.

For poor Miss Ophelia, already burdened with the care of a lot of little blacks, it was hard to understand why fate had brought this imp of darkness into her life.

But, being a good Christian woman, she bowed to the inevitable and promised to do her best with the child.

"How old are you, Topsy?" she asked, kindly.

"Dunno, missis," said Topsy, showing all her white teeth.

"Didn't anybody ever tell you? Who was your mother?"

"Nevah had none!" answered the child with another grin.

"Never had a mother? Why, Topsy, what do you mean? Where were you born?"

"Nevah was born!" replied the little imp, still grinning, and all the questions

Miss Ophelia could bring to bear failed to make the child own that she ever had a mother or had ever been born.

"Have you ever heard about God, Topsy?" asked Miss Ophelia, but the child had no answer. She didn't know what the good lady meant.

"Do you know who made you?"

"Nobody, as I know on," replied the child; "I 'spect I jest growed."

The poor child knew nothing but how to "fetch" water, wash dishes and rub knives, so she told Miss Ophelia, and afterward, when caught stealing, she didn't even know it was wrong to steal. When compelled to confess, she told of stealing things that she never stole at all, explaining that "Missis told me to 'fess and I couldn't think o' nothin' else to 'fess." So she told of stealing earrings and burning them up, when, as a matter of fact, little Eva St. Clare had them in her ears at the time.

There was something in the black child that touched the kindly heart of little Eva, who, though but a child herself, had, by reason of long illness, grown old beyond her years.

"Poor Topsy," she said kindly, "you need never steal again. You are to be taken care of now. I'd give you anything of mine rather than have you steal it."

It almost seemed as though the black child understood the bond of sympathy held out to her, but she could only blink and rub her eyes. It was the first kindly word she had ever understood and it caused a queer feeling in her heart. Being pure and gentle herself, Eva soon exer-

cised an influence on little black Topsy that changed her into a rare jewel.

Being smart and active she soon learned the ways of negroes of the better class. Of course, she would have to play at times and did some very silly things, like pulling off the pillow-cases and butting at the pillows with her woolly head, and sometimes feathers would creep through and stick in her crinkled hair. And she would dress the bolster up in Miss Ophelia's night clothes and, when scolded, would ask to be "whipped like old missis allers whipped me," a thing Miss Ophelia could not bring herself to do.

As in all cases where once a person has been caught stealing, there is a lurking suspicion against them. So it was with Topsy, who, when little Eva was slowly passing from this world, used to pick flowers and take them to Eva's bedside.

One day she was caught, and not until Eva herself informed the captors that she had told Topsy to pick the flowers and

bring them to her was the little black girl released. The next time suspicion fell on the child was after Eva's sad end, and the little darkey was seen to hide something quickly in the bosom of her dress as some one approached. What do you suppose was hidden? A curl from little Eva's hair and a tiny Bible—both had been given Topsy by the little white girl before her death. After this episode Topsy became the special favorite of Mr. St. Clare, who declared that the child must never again

be molested.   Strange to say, when Topsy
grew up she became a teacher in far-away
Africa, among people of her own kind and
color.

Lightning Source UK Ltd.
Milton Keynes UK
UKHW022319080223
416651UK00001B/27